WHY THIS IS AN EASY READER

- This story has been carefully written to keep the young reader's interest high.

- It is told in a simple, open style, with a strong rhythm that adds enjoyment both to reading aloud and silent reading.

- There is a very high percentage of words repeated. It is this skillful repetition which helps the child to read independently. Seeing words again and again, he "practices" the vocabulary he knows, and learns with ease the words that are new.

- Only 176 different words have been used, with plurals and root words counted once.

    Over one-half of the words in this story have been used at least three times.

    Over one-fourth of the words have been used at least six times.

    Some words have been used 30, 39 and 56 times.

ABOUT THIS STORY

- The mouse hero of this story lives in the miniature world that so enchants young readers—and his mouse house and toy train ride will charm them. But they will also understand his life-sized problem of loneliness.

- There is another Easy Reader about Little Gray Mouse. It is called THE SURPRISE IN THE STORY BOOK.

LITTLE GRAY MOUSE AND THE TRAIN

Story by SARA ASHERON
Pictures by CLAUDINE NANKIVEL
Editorial Consultant: LILIAN MOORE

WONDER BOOKS
A Division of Grosset & Dunlap, Inc.
New York, N.Y. 10010

Introduction

These books are meant to help the young reader discover what a delightful experience reading can be. The stories are such fun that they urge the child to try his new reading skills. They are so easy to read that they will encourage and strengthen him as a reader.

The adult will notice that the sentences aren't too long, the words aren't too hard, and the skillful repetition is like a helping hand. What the child will feel is: "This is a good story—and I can read it myself!"

For some children, the best way to meet these stories may be to hear them read aloud at first. Others, who are better prepared to read on their own, may need a little help in the beginning—help that is best given freely. Youngsters who have more experience in reading alone—whether in first or second or third grade—will have the immediate joy or reading "all by myself."

These books have been planned to help all young readers grow—in their pleasure in books and in their power to read them.

Lilian Moore
Specialist in Reading
Formerly of Division of Instructional Research,
New York City Board of Education

Little Gray Mouse
was feeling sad.
"What is the matter with me?"
he said to himself.

8

He looked around.

"I live in the best house

on the street," he said.

"I LIKE this house."

He looked around.

"I have a cozy little mouse house
in the wall," he said.

"I LIKE my mouse house."

"I have good things to eat, too,"
said Little Gray Mouse.
"Cake crumbs—
Bread crumbs—
Jelly crumbs—"

A boy lived in the house.

"I LIKE the boy," said the mouse

to himself.

A girl lived there, too.

"I like the little girl,"

said the mouse,

"and the mother and father, too."

A cat lived in the house next door.

But there was a bell on the cat.

Little Gray Mouse was not afraid

of THAT cat.

"What is the matter with me?"

said Little Gray Mouse to himself.

"I feel so sad.

What do I want?"

One day Little Gray Mouse
ran downstairs.
He ran down
to get something to eat.

What a surprise!

There was a little brown mouse.

"Hello," said the little

brown mouse.

"My name is Squeaky."

"Hello, Squeaky,"

said Little Gray Mouse.

"I am looking for a new home,"
said Squeaky.
"Do you like living here?"

"Oh, yes," said Gray Mouse.

"It's very nice.

There's a boy

and a girl

and a father

and a mother.

But they are quiet people."

"Good!" said Squeaky

"I like quiet people!"

"Do you have cats here?"

asked Squeaky.

"Too many cats live
in my old house!"

"A cat lives next door,"

said Little Gray Mouse.

"But there is a bell on him."

"Good!" said Squeaky.

"I like cats with bells!"

23

"I live upstairs in the boy's room,"
said Little Gray Mouse.

"Come and see."

They ran upstairs to the boy's room.

"See," said Gray Mouse.

"I live here . . .

And there is a nice mouse house
over there across the room.
You can live there."

"In a BOY'S room?" asked Squeaky.
He made a face.

"Oh, this boy goes out to play
all day," Gray Mouse told him.

"And he eats good things here.
I find
cake crumbs
and candy crumbs
and bread crumbs with jelly—"

"Yummy!" said Squeaky.

"That's for me!"

So Squeaky came to live
in the nice little mouse house
across the room.

Now Little Gray Mouse had

someone to play with.

Now he did not feel sad.

"I just wanted a friend,"

he said to himself.

"THAT was the matter with me!"

The mouse friends had fun.
Every day the boy ran out
to play.

Then Squeaky
and Little Gray Mouse
ran out to play, too.

They played

here and there

in the boy's room.

They played
upstairs

and downstairs.

Sometimes Squeaky ran
across the room to have lunch
with Little Gray Mouse.

Sometimes Gray Mouse ran
across the room to have lunch
with Squeaky.
Gray Mouse liked that best of all.

One day some boys and girls

came to the house.

So many boys and girls!

"What's going on here?"

asked Squeaky.

But Little Gray Mouse did not know.

The children sat down

to eat.

They had cake and candy.

So did Gray Mouse!

So did Squeaky!

Then the children played games.

What was that?
Squeaky ran to his mouse house.
So did Little Gray Mouse.

"Maybe the children will go home
soon," Gray Mouse said to himself.
"Maybe the boy will go out
to play."

The children did go home soon.
But the boy did not go out
to play.

He came up to his room.

The father came, too.

Then the boy and his father played

with a train.

They made the train go

TOOT!

TOOT!

They made the train go

around and around the room.

"Maybe they will go away soon,"
said Little Gray Mouse to himself.
"It's time for lunch.
It's time for me to go
across the room to Squeaky.
I hate to be late."

But the boy and his father
played and played with the train.
Then the father went downstairs.

But the boy did not go away.

He went on playing

with the train.

Soon his friend came

to play with him.

"Silly boys!" said Gray Mouse
to himself.
"Go out and play.
It's not good for you to play
in the house all day!"
But the boys went on playing
with the train.
They made the train go.
They made it stop.
GO.

TOOT!

TOOT!

STOP.

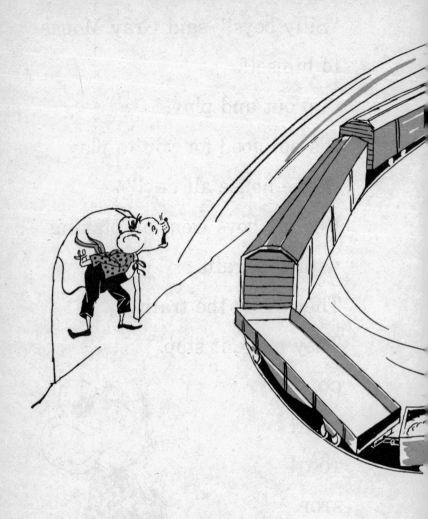

"I do hate to be late,"

said Little Gray Mouse.

He looked out at the little train.

48

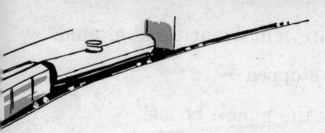

Around and around went the train.

Stop.

Go.

Stop.

The train went around and around.

Then it stopped—

right by the mouse house!

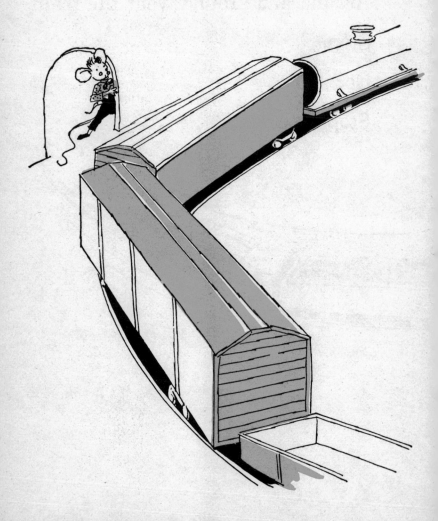

"OH!" said Little Gray Mouse.

"I know what I can do!"

Little Gray Mouse gave

a little run

a big jump

and a little hop.

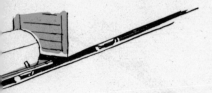

And there he was on the train!

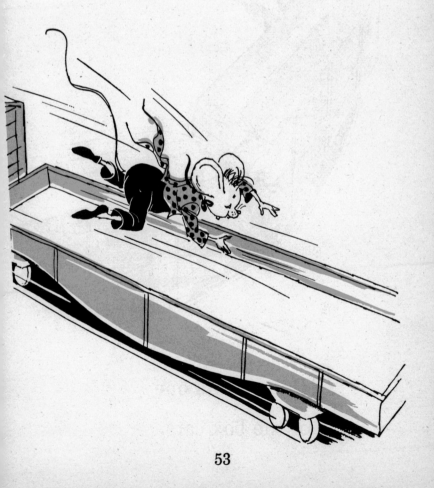

He ran into one
of the box cars.

The box car had a door.

Gray Mouse made himself
very little in the box car.

TOOT!

TOOT!

The train began to go—

Around and around and around.

Gray Mouse was a little afraid.

But then he began to have fun.

Stop.

Go.

TOOT!

TOOT!

The train stopped.

Little Gray Mouse looked out.

He was right at Squeaky's house!

He looked around.

The boys did not see him.

He gave a little run,

a big jump

and a little hop.

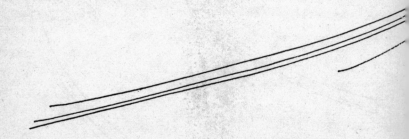

What a surprise for Squeaky!

There was Little Gray Mouse.

He had come for lunch after all.

"I hate to be so late,"

said Little Gray Mouse.

"You see, I had to come by train."

CHOOSE FROM THESE EASY READERS